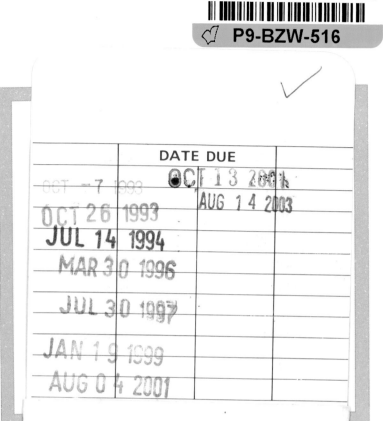

For Cornelia — J.O'C.

To Darryl and my parents — L.S.L.

Copyright © 1993 by Girl Scouts of the United States of America. All rights reserved. Published by Grosset & Dunlap, Inc., a member of The Putnam & Grosset Group, New York, in cooperation with Girl Scouts of the United States of America. Published simultaneously in Canada. Printed in the U.S.A.

Library of Congress Cataloging-in-Publication Data
O'Connor, Jane.
    Corrie's secret pal / by Jane O'Connor ; illustrated by Laurie Struck Long.
        p.    cm. — (Here come the Brownies)
    Summary: A lonely new student finds friends and adventures after joining a Brownie Girl Scout troop.
    [1. Girl Scouts—Fiction.   2. Moving, Household—Fiction.
3. Friendship—Fiction.]   I. Long, Laurie Struck, ill.   II. Title.   III. Series.
PZ7.0222Co   1993
[E]—dc20                                                                    92-35602

ISBN 0-448-40160-6 (pbk.)        A  B  C  D  E  F  G  H  I  J
ISBN 0-448-40161-4 (GB)          A  B  C  D  E  F  G  H  I  J

Friendship bracelet directions reprinted by permission of Grosset & Dunlap from *Knot Now!*, written and illustrated by Margaret A. Hartelius, copyright © 1992 by Margaret A. Hartelius.

# HERE COME THE BROWNIES
## A Brownie Girl Scout Book

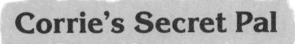

## Corrie's Secret Pal

By Jane O'Connor
Illustrated by Laurie Struck Long

Grosset & Dunlap • New York
In association with GIRL SCOUTS OF THE USA

# 1

"Just give it a try," Corrie's mom had said. "Your Aunt Maria always loved being a Brownie. I think it will be a wonderful way for you to make more friends."

"More friends? What you mean is *some* friends," Corrie said. "I don't have any friends here."

"We only moved a month ago," Corrie's mom pointed out. "It takes time to make new friends. But you will. I know."

How could her mom know that for sure? Corrie wondered. Grown-ups always said stuff like that.

"So will you? Will you give the troop a try?"

Corrie nodded.

Today right after school was her first Brownie Girl Scout meeting.

"Have a good weekend," Mrs. Fujikawa was telling everybody in 2-B. "Bus people, please line up in the hall."

The bus people filed outside.

"Brownies, you may go down to the lunchroom. Wait there for your troop leader."

Besides Corrie, about seven girls stood up. Corrie was surprised to see so many. She had figured Marsha and Amy were Brownies.

They wore their uniforms to school each
Friday. But Krissy A. was a Brownie. So
were Krissy S. and Jo Ann and Lauren.
And the really tall girl whose name she
always forgot.

"Corrie, where are you going? You're not in Brownies," Amy said. She didn't say it in a mean way. Still, it made Corrie feel like she didn't belong. That was a feeling she had a lot lately.

"My mom just signed me up," Corrie explained to Amy. "I'm giving it a try."

"It's so fun," Amy told her. "We go ice-skating. We sell cookies. We learn about nature and science and make all kinds of stuff. We get to go on sleepovers." Amy caught her breath. Then she went on. "And what's really cool is the camping trip. That's for a whole weekend! Last year it rained and rained practically the whole time. But I still loved it. I can't wait until we go again."

"This is my third year in Girl Scouts,"

Marsha informed Corrie. Then she slung an arm around Lauren. And they dashed downstairs.

Marsha and Lauren. It was like they had "best friends" stamped all over them. Each Monday everybody in 2-B had to write a paragraph about their weekend. Then they had to read it to the class. Marsha's and Lauren's paragraphs were always about the fun stuff they had done together.

As Corrie headed for the lunchroom, she touched her heart locket. Inside was a picture of Jen. Jen was Corrie's best friend from her old neighborhood. The picture had been taken right after Jen got over chicken pox. There were red marks all over her face.

Still, Corrie treasured the picture. How she wished Jen was here now to start Brownies with her.

In the lunchroom Corrie sat down at a long table. Over it was a sign that said "BROWNIE GIRL SCOUTS MEET HERE" with an arrow pointing down.

"Who's got snack kaper? I'm starved!" Amy asked. She was busy showing everyone how she could roll her eyes back until only the whites showed.

"I'm nearly done with the Safety Try-It," Marsha was saying.

"Remember that kid with the really long hair? The one who flew up last spring?" another Brownie was telling the table. "I saw her at the mall. She was getting her ears pierced!"

Snack kaper? Safety Try-It? A girl who flew up? What were they all talking about? Corrie did not have a clue.

"You must be Corrie."

Corrie looked up.

"I'm your fearless leader," said a lady with red hair. "My name is Jean Quinones. But everybody just calls me Mrs. Q."

"I think I have all the stuff here," Corrie said. She fished in her backpack and handed her forms and slips to Mrs. Q.

"Fine." Mrs. Q. checked through everything. Then she bent down beside Corrie. "I'm so happy to have you in our troop. I'm sure you are going to be a wonderful Girl Scout. We have a lot of fun here...and you'll learn to do lots of new things."

Corrie nodded. Being a Brownie Girl Scout did sound like fun. The trouble was that this was one more *new* thing. And there was too much *new* right now. New house. New town. New school.

Corrie nibbled on one of the apple slices that were being passed out by the tall girl whose name she didn't know.

"There's peanut butter to smush on it," the tall girl told Corrie.

"Thanks. I'm not that hungry." Corrie smiled. The tall girl smiled back. Both her front teeth were in. They were very big and very white.

"I started to bake cookies. But our puppy sheds a lot. All this dog hair got in the batter. Sick!" Then the tall girl covered her mouth. Mrs. Q. was raising her right arm.

"That's the quiet sign," the tall girl said. She raised her hand, too. "When your hand goes up, your mouth goes shut and you raise your hand for someone else to see."

"Ladies, please settle down," Mrs Q. was saying. "We want to welcome Corrie to our troop today. Some of you know Corrie already. But I would still like to go around the table and have each girl say her name."

BROWNIE GIRL SCOUTS MEET HERE ⇩

"Sarah," said the tall girl with the big front teeth. So *that* was her name.

Then Mrs. Q. asked everyone to say the Pledge of Allegiance and the Girl Scout Promise. Lucky for Corrie, Mrs. Q. had a big index card with all the words on it. After the Girl Scout Promise, everybody sat down in a circle on the floor.

"This is our Brownie Ring where we talk over stuff," Sarah whispered to Corrie. "And plan things."

Today Mrs. Q. asked if the girls would like to tell their own thoughts about what Girl Scouting meant to them.

"Aw! We've already done that. Do we have to?" a few girls complained.

"Is that how Brownie Girl Scouts behave?" Mrs. Q. asked. The girls who had said "Aw" shook their heads reluctantly.

"Remember. We have a new girl with us today," Mrs. Q. added.

Amy raised her hand. "What if we do our skit again? The one we did for new Brownies at the first meeting?"

Mrs. Q. looked at the big clock above the stack of lunch trays. "Good idea, Amy. If we hurry, we'll have time. Krissy S., please get our scripts and costumes from the teachers' room. Everybody take the same parts."

# 2

In a short time, everyone was ready to start. Mrs. Q. sat beside Corrie. She rested a hand on Corrie's back. It felt nice. Like something her mother would do.

Then Amy stood up. She cleared her throat dramatically. "The critics loved it. *You* loved it. So now—back by popular demand—is the show everyone's talking about. The smash hit of the season. The—"

"Let's get on with it, Amy." Mrs. Q. smiled.

" 'The Brownie Story!' " Amy stretched out the word "Brownie." Then she looked down at her script and started to read.

"Long, long ago a little girl lived at the edge of the woods with her father, who was a poor tailor, and her grandmother."

Amy went on telling how the little girl never helped out. All she did was stuff she wanted to do.

"What this house needs is a Brownie," said Marsha. Marsha played the part of the old grandmother. She carried a cane. And she read her script in a shaky voice. She was pretty good, Corrie thought.

"Granny...what...is...a...Brownie?" asked the kid who was playing the little girl. She was missing a front tooth. And she read each word separately and carefully. "What... did...she...look...like?"

"We never saw her. But she swept the floor. She set the table. She cleaned the whole house," Granny Marsha said.

"Did she get any monkey?" asked the little girl. "Oops. I mean *money*."

"No, my dear," said the granny. "Brownies always help for love."

Corrie listened while the skit went on. The little girl wanted to meet a real live Brownie. So one night she went into the

woods. She asked the Wise Old Owl where she could find a Brownie.

The Wise Old Owl had on a paper bag mask that was a little crumpled and a pair of cardboard wings. She told the little girl to go to the pond. If she said a special magic charm and looked into the pond, she would see a Brownie.

But when the little girl did this, she only saw herself in the pond.

"But...I...am...not...a...Brownie."
The little girl held out her arms and
shrugged.

"Are you sure?" came the muffled voice
of the owl from inside the paper bag mask.
"Anyone can be a Brownie. You just have to
help out."

The little girl's mouth formed into a
big O.

"Now I see!" she read slowly. "I can be a
Brownie, too!"

"So the little girl went home," Amy said.
"And she cleaned up the house. Every inch
of it."

The little girl was holding a broom now.
She raced all around pretending to clean.
Corrie giggled. It looked like a movie when
everything gets speeded up.

"When the poor tailor and the old granny came downstairs, were they surprised," read Amy.

Marsha hobbled out again with the poor tailor. Their jaws dropped open. They rubbed their eyes a lot.

"Who did this?" asked the granny.

"A Brownie!" sang the little girl. "I am the Brownie!"

"And so she was," Amy said. "The end."

Everybody clapped. Amy bowed so low that the ribbon on the end of her braid touched the floor.

Some mothers and babysitters were already by the door. So Mrs. Q. rushed everybody back into a circle.

"Sorry, no time for songs. Just the friendship squeeze."

The what? thought Corrie.

The tall girl—Sarah—saw the look on Corrie's face.

"Just cross your arms like this. Then hold my hand and Lauren's. After you feel Lauren squeeze your hand, squeeze mine. That's how you pass it along."

"I'll start," Mrs. Q. said. "And we'll go to my right."

From one girl to the next, the friendship squeeze rippled around the circle.

As soon as Corrie felt Lauren's squeeze, she gave a squeeze to Sarah. It was nice. It made Corrie feel like a link in a big chain. She just hoped her hands weren't hot and sweaty.

"If you want, you can borrow my Brownie Girl Scout Handbook," Sarah told Corrie as they went to get their things. "It tells you everything about Brownies. I can drop it off at your house."

"Thanks," Corrie said. "You want to come over tomorrow? You could stay and play." It would be the first time anyone from 2-B had been to her new house. Only Jen and other old friends of Corrie's had come to play. And now they had to come by car.

"I can't on Saturday," Sarah said. "I help out my dad. He's a vet. But I think Sunday is okay. . . . I'll call and let you know. Oh. There's my mom! I've got to go."

"Remember. Next week is our junk swap," Mrs. Q. called out to everybody. "I'll send a note to your classrooms with more info."

Corrie found her backpack and then found her brother. He was outside in the hallway. On Fridays her mom always had to work late at the newspaper. So it was Rob's job to take Corrie home.

Rob was deep into the latest issue of "Terminator Ants." He peered over his comic book at Corrie. "Where's your uniform? Where are the medals? Did you sign up for life?"

"It's not like that." Rob was okay. But he liked to tease too much.

Corrie wacked Rob with her backpack. She ducked before he could get her back. Then she ran down the hallway.

"Hey, Corrie. Something is hanging out of your backpack," Rob called.

"Oh, I'm sure." Corrie was not falling for that one.

"Okay. Your loss. See if I care."

Corrie jerked her head around fast. No joke! Something <u>was</u> falling out of her backpack. It was a ribbon. A pretty orange hair ribbon.

Orange and brown were Brownie Girl Scout colors. Corrie knew that. But she didn't have any Brownie stuff. Not yet. So the ribbon had to belong to someone else.

She was about to go back and give it to Mrs. Q. when she saw there was a note. It was written on school paper.

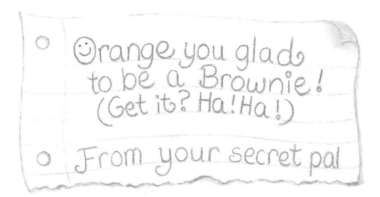

It looked like somebody had scribbled the note fast. Mrs. Q. maybe. But the fat curly writing looked more like a kid's. Could it be Sarah? She seemed very nice. That's probably just who it was.

"Gotcha!" he cried.

Robby pounced and gave Corrie a good wack with his backpack.

# 3

"Of course she can come over!" Mom said. "Maybe she'd like to stay for dinner. Why don't you call Susan and ask?"

"It's Sarah, Ma. Not Susan." Corrie knew her mother wanted her to make new friends. Corrie did too. But she wished her mother wouldn't make such a big deal out of it.

Sarah arrived after lunch on Sunday with her Brownie Girl Scout Handbook. "Keep it as long as you want," she told Corrie.

"Thanks," Corrie said. "Hey. See what I have on?" She twirled around so Sarah could see the secret pal ribbon in her hair.

"What?"

"This ribbon." Corrie said, pointing. "Orange you glad to be a Brownie?"

"Yes. Sure I am," was all Sarah said. So Corrie didn't push it. If her secret pal wanted to stay secret, that was okay with her.

Corrie and Sarah went upstairs. Sarah didn't want to play with Corrie's Barbies. She did not like dressing up either. Or pretending to be a ballerina, like Jen did. Sarah wanted to go outside and look for worms and slugs. But it was raining very hard. And Corrie was not too crazy about worms anyway.

They ended up playing hide-and-go-seek. And when they got tired of that, they drew pictures at the kitchen table. Corrie drew a pink unicorn with a purple horn.

"Ooh. You're so good!" Sarah said.

Corrie was used to hearing that.

"Thank you," she said modestly. Unicorns were her specialty. "I like your pig, too."

Sarah laughed. "It's a dog."

"Oops! Sorry!" Corrie clapped her hand over her mouth.

"It's okay. I know I stink. It's supposed to be my puppy. Her name is Muffin."

Sarah pulled a locket out from under her T-shirt. It was like the one Corrie wore.

"See." Sarah popped open her locket. There was a photo inside. All Corrie could make out were two black eyes and a tongue.

"Muffin jumped when the flash went off. So this picture isn't very good." Sarah closed her locket. "She is very cute in real life. I also have a cat named Norma. And

three hamsters named Huey, Dewey, and Louie. And lots of fish. I am an animal person. You'll have to come over and meet them."

Corrie's mom was making cupcakes and heard that. She was a newspaper reporter. There was not much that she missed.

The minute Sarah left, Corrie's mom said, "She seems like such a nice girl."

"She is," Corrie said. She liked Sarah. And she wanted to go to her house. But Sarah wasn't like Jen. Corrie could tell that. And Corrie bet her mom could too.

# 4

On Monday Corrie found a big oatmeal cookie in her lunch bag. It was from her secret pal. On Wednesday there was an envelope taped to her cubby. Inside was a friendship bracelet made from brown and orange string. The note with it said, "Your secret pal strikes again!" in fat curly writing.

Corrie put on the bracelet. She went up to Sarah. Sarah was thumb wrestling with David, a boy in their class. Corrie waited until Sarah won. Then she dangled her arm in front of Sarah. "Like my new bracelet?"

"Oh! I tried to make one of those once. But mine was a mess." Again Sarah was acting like she didn't know a thing about the surprise present. Still, Corrie was pretty sure Sarah was her secret pal. Sarah was nice. And she was a Brownie Girl Scout. Being a secret pal was just the kind of thing Brownies did. Corrie knew that from the Brownie Girl Scout Handbook. She read some of it every night.

Corrie learned that kapers were troop jobs. Try-Its were patches Brownies got for doing Brownie-type stuff, like having a pick-up-litter day at school. Or learning to cook foods from foreign lands. And flying up was when a Brownie Girl Scout was ready to become a Junior Girl Scout.

The more Corrie read, the more she

wanted to be a Brownie. She taught herself
the Girl Scout Promise. She knew the words
to the Brownie Smile Song. And she learned
the Girl Scout Law.

Helping out was a real big thing with the
Girl Scouts. So Corrie cleaned up her whole
room. Without being asked. And she did a
load of laundry all by herself. Her mom
wasn't even mad that somehow all the
underwear had turned a little green.

Corrie was looking forward to the next Brownie meeting. It sounded like a lot of fun.

Mrs. Fujikawa had passed out a note from Mrs. Q. to all the Brownies in 2-B. It said:

Tired of your toys?
Bored with your board games?
Then it's time to recycle them! Bring all your old stuff to our next meeting. You can trade and also help give toys to kids who don't have many.
See you Friday.

Mrs. Q.

P.S. Make sure your parents say it's okay to bring your things.

For every trade they made, the girls were going to put something from their piles into a box to give to other kids.

Corrie had three shopping bags full of stuff with her. Old doll clothes. Some books. A pair of roller skates that were too small. Most of a tea party dish set. Chinese checkers. A piggy bank with a chipped tail that said "I ♥ New York." No. On second thought, Corrie was going to keep that. Jen had given it to her.

Corrie had also made a big sign.

"Corrie's Swap Shop" it said in fancy letters. Corrie filled in the C and both S's with gold glitter.

Underneath Corrie wrote:

WHAT'S OLD TO ME IS NEW TO YOU!

She drew a toy box with felt markers. She filled it with teddy bears and dolls. It was half open so it looked sort of like a treasure chest.

Now she was ready.

# 5

At the troop meeting Mrs. Q. asked each girl to put her things out on one of the lunchroom tables. Amy was at the table next to Corrie. She watched Corrie tape up her sign.

"That's cool. I wish I was good in art like you. I see you draw those unicorns in free time. You draw better than anybody in 2-B. Honest."

Corrie was about to tell Amy that she

would draw a unicorn. Just for her. But a couple of other girls came over. They tugged on Amy's arm. "Come on," they said. "Let's check out all the stuff."

That's what everybody did.

Corrie went around from table to table.

Sarah had brought in lots of books about nature. Also a rock collection in a shoe box. And a magnifying glass with a crack in it. Krissy S. had dress-up stuff. Amy had a magic set that was missing a few tricks.

By the end of the meeting, everyone had a big bag of new-to-them toys to take home. And there was a giant carton of stuff to give away to other kids. Corrie had traded everything except some doll clothes. She had been so busy making deals, she could not remember half the things she got.

When she got home, she dumped everything on her bed. There were four mystery books that had belonged to Krissy S. Amy's magic set. Lots of scented markers that Sarah promised weren't dried up. And a pretty pink jewelry box that had been Marsha's.

Corrie opened the jewelry box. A little ballerina popped up. Once the jewelry box had played music and the ballerina could spin around. Now it was broken. But Corrie didn't care. It was still beautiful.

Corrie pulled out the drawer in the jewelry box.

It wasn't empty. Marsha must have forgotten to clean it out.

There was a long strip of snapshots of Marsha and Lauren. The kind you take in a little booth. In one Marsha had her eyes crossed. In another she was holding two fingers behind Lauren's head giving her "bunny ears."

Besides the snapshots Corrie saw a letter. Corrie was sure Marsha would want the pictures back. The letter, too.

Corrie knew she wasn't supposed to read other people's letters. It certainly wasn't something a Brownie would do. But this one wasn't folded up or anything. So it really wasn't like snooping. Before she could stop herself, Corrie saw what it said.

A NOTE FROM AMY...

Marsha,
The party is at 6:00, on the 15th. Everybody is coming. Don't let you-know-who find out!!!! ☺

Amy had also written down the date of the party on the note. It was going to be next Friday.

Corrie's tummy did a flip-flop. She closed the drawer of the jewelry box. She had no right to feel bad. After all, she hardly knew Amy. So what if she was having a party and hadn't asked her?

Still, all of a sudden Corrie didn't feel like looking at the new-to-her stuff. She pushed it off her bed. She wanted her old stuff back. She wanted her old room back too. In her old house. She wanted to be back in her old school with Jen and her old friends.

That's all there was to it!

# 6

"Well, I guess *somebody* likes me,"
Corrie thought. She was holding a Brownie
bookmark with an orange tassel. She had
found it in her desk. It looked like her secret
pal had struck again.

Corrie turned around in her seat. She held
up the bookmark. "It's you, isn't it?"
Corrie was about to say to Sarah.

Sarah sat a row behind Corrie. But Sarah
was not at her desk. Sarah was out sick.
Sarah must have put the bookmark there

last Friday, Corrie figured. Right after school was over. That had to be it. Well, from now on, Corrie was going to keep a close eye on Sarah. Next time she was going to catch her in the act!

On the lunch line Corrie stood right behind Amy, Marsha, and Lauren.

Corrie tapped Marsha on the back.

"Um...I think these are yours," she said. She held out the snapshots. "I found them in your old ballerina jewelry box."

"Oh, gosh! Thanks," said Marsha. "I forgot they were there."

Corrie hoped Marsha had forgotten about the note, too. Corrie had torn it up into lots of little pieces.

Lauren looked at the pictures too. "Oh! I look so dumb!" she shrieked. "I can't believe how dumb I look!"

At lunch Corrie usually sat with Sarah. But today Amy asked Corrie to sit with her. Marsha and Lauren and Jo Ann were there too.

They talked about how hard math was. And who had lost the most teeth. And which boy in their class was the most disgusting. Corrie found out that Amy's father worked at the same newspaper as her mother.

"He writes about people who just died. Sick, huh?" said Amy.

Corrie's mom wrote human interest stories. That was stuff like Fourth of July hot-dog eating contests and people who found out they had a long lost twin. Everybody agreed. Human interest sounded way better than dead people.

Corrie was sorry when lunch was over.

These girls were nice. Amy most of all. Amy could stick two fingers in her mouth and whistle so loud it made your ears ring. She was double-jointed. And she had a trapeze. Right in her room!

"You can come over and try it," Amy told Corrie.

Amy was so nice. Corrie half-expected Amy to come over and say, "Look. I'm having a party this Friday. I know it's late to ask. But can you come?"

That didn't happen though.

Two days later Sarah came back to school. She'd had a bad cold. Her nose was still very runny.

"If you are better on Friday, do you want to come for a sleepover?" Corrie asked her. "I got a note saying there's no Brownies this week. So you could come home with me after school."

"Uh, sorry. I'm busy that night." Sarah sounded nervous. She sniffed and rubbed her nose. "And...and I have stuff I have to do right after school...but thanks!"

Corrie didn't say anything more. Sarah was going to Amy's party, too!

Sarah wasn't friends with Amy. No more than Corrie was. Corrie was probably the only girl in 2-B who wasn't invited!

# 7

It was late Friday afternoon. Everyone must be at Amy's house by now. They were probably all taking turns on Amy's trapeze and seeing who could whistle the loudest.

Corrie lay on the sofa. She did not feel like reading. She did not feel like drawing. She turned on the TV to drown out the tape her brother was listening to.

A soap opera was on.

"Things will get better between us,

Tiffany," a man said to a sobbing woman.

The woman sobbed even harder. "Oh, Clark. If only we could turn back the hands of time."

"Any signs of life here?" It was Corrie's mom.

She came bursting through the front door. She had her briefcase in one hand. And a pizza box cradled in the other. "Corrie, come on. You know I don't like you to watch those silly soaps. You're going to rot your brain."

But then Corrie's mom stopped scolding. She saw how sad Corrie looked. She put down the pizza and her briefcase.

"Oh, sweetie. Why the long face?"

Corrie let out a gusty sigh.

"I wish I could turn back the hands of time."

Corrie's mom did not laugh. She was still in her coat. But she sat down beside Corrie. "I know there is a lot to get used to. And you're being a champ. You really are."

"Somebody in my class is having a party tonight." There. She had said it. "Yours truly was not invited. I told you I don't have any friends."

Corrie's mom took her hand. "Don't be

so sure. You *do* have friends. I'm just sure you do." She brushed a strand of hair away from Corrie's forehead. "Now let's dig into this pizza. I told Jean Quinones that we'd be over at six o'clock."

"Who?" asked Corrie.

"Jean Quinones. Your troop leader."

"Oh. Mrs. Q.!" said Corrie. She was not used to hearing Mrs. Q. called by her full name. "Why are we going there?"

"I thought I told you. She called the other day. She has a Brownie uniform that she thinks will fit you. It belonged to one of her girls."

"No kidding!" Corrie pictured herself in a Brownie blouse and jumper. Maybe there would be a beanie to go with them.

Corrie perked up a bit. She helped her

mom and her brother work their way through a large pizza. Then they piled in the van. Her brother got dropped off at the movie theater in the mall.

From the mall it was just a short drive to Mrs. Q.'s house.

# 8

They rang the bell. Corrie could hear voices inside. Laughing too.

"Hello there!" Mrs. Q. held open the door. "We've been waiting for you."

Corrie did not have time to think about what Mrs. Q.'s words meant.

"Surprise!" everyone shouted.

Her whole Brownie troop was there! Amy. Sarah. Marsha. Lauren. Everybody.

"I don't get it," Corrie said.

"Your Brownie friends planned this all on their own," Corrie's mom said. "I wanted to tell you about it when I saw how sad you were. But I didn't want to spoil the surprise."

"Your mom told me that you know the Girl Scout Promise," Mrs. Q. said. "And you understand what it means to be a Brownie Girl Scout."

Corrie nodded. She did.

"Then you are ready to become a Brownie. Tonight. We always have a ceremony. That makes it special."

"So we're having a party," Sarah chimed in. "A party for you!"

Now it all became clear. Corrie remembered the note she had torn up. The one Amy wrote to Marsha. It said, "Be there at 6:00. Don't tell you-know-who."

Well, "there" was right here. Now! At

Mrs. Q.'s house. And Corrie was the "you-know-who." The note had been about this party!

Corrie was lost for words. "Thanks... Thanks so much" she sputtered.

"You're very welcome," Mrs. Q. told Corrie. "If you look, you will see all the food is brown or orange. That was the girls' idea, too."

"I've never had a surprise party before. My grandma did. But that was when she turned seventy!" Corrie felt like a big wave had knocked her over.

"Have a brownie," Sarah said. "I baked them." Then she whispered, "There's no dog hair in them. I swear!"

Corrie had a brownie. She also had a bunch of cheese twists and some chocolate-covered pretzels.

Then Mrs. Q. got down to business. She handed Corrie a pile of folded-up clothes. The uniform!

Corrie licked all the cheese dust off her fingers. Then she went and changed in Mrs. Q.'s bedroom.

Corrie came out.

"Ta da!" Corrie tried to sound the way Amy would.

"You look great!" Sarah said.

Corrie caught a look at herself in the mirror over the sofa. Corrie had to admit it. She did look great. Older, too. Corrie bet she could pass for a third grader.

Corrie's mom helped Mrs. Q. take down the big mirror. They put it on the floor. Then the girls got plants from all over the house and arranged them around the mirror.

"This is supposed to be the pond in the

story of the Brownies," Mrs. Q. explained.
"Everybody please have a seat now." She
waited a moment. Then Mrs. Q. cleared her
throat. "Tonight is a special night. Corrie is
becoming one of our sisters in Girl Scouting.
Who would like to bring Corrie into our
troop?"

Amy's hand shot up.

"All right . . . Amy."

Amy stepped forward. She cleared her
throat. Corrie expected her to come out
with some joke. Or make a funny face. But
Amy didn't.

"I would like to bring Corrie into our
troop," she said. "I hope she has fun and—
uh—learns neat stuff. Like I have."

Then Amy put her hands around Corrie's
waist. It tickled. But Corrie did not laugh.

Amy twisted Corrie around three times

while she said the words to the magic charm.

"Twist me and turn me and show me the elf.

I looked in the pond and saw—"

Corrie bent down. She looked into the pond mirror. She finished the magic charm.

"Myself!" she said.

Everybody clapped. Amy stuck two

fingers in her mouth and whistled loudly.
Sarah smiled and gave Corrie a little hug.

Mom had said all her Brownie friends
had planned this party. *All her Brownie
friends.* That sounded so nice.

Corrie peered into the pond mirror again.
The Corrie that looked back at her looked
like a new Corrie. She felt like all sorts of
new things—good new things—were going
to happen to her. It was a little like opening
a brand-new box of crayons. Corrie always
knew she'd make lots of great drawings
with them. She just didn't know what they
would look like yet.

Amy poked Corrie in the ribs.

"Orange you glad to be a Brownie?"
Amy asked.

"What?" Corrie's mouth dropped open.
"It's you! You're my secret pal."

"The one and only!" Amy bowed. She was wearing an orange ribbon on her braid. Just like the one she had given Corrie. "I moved here last year. Being new is—" Amy pretended to stick a finger down her throat. "So? Orange you glad to be a Brownie?"

"Yes!" said Corrie.

And she was.

# Girl Scout Ways

It's easy to be a secret pal. First, pick a person. Then surprise them with little notes or presents— like a friendship bracelet. Here's one that's easy to make. Choose two different colors, just like Amy did when she made Corrie's!

**1.** You will need two 15-inch strings of one color (A), and two 15-inch strings of another color (B).

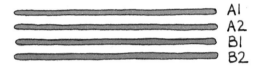

- AI
- A2
- BI
- B2

**2.** Tie them together with a knot near the top.

- AI
- A2
- BI
- B2

**3.** Tape the loop to a tabletop.

AI  A2  BI  B2

AI  A2  B2  BI

**4.** Arrange the colors like this: $A_1$, $A_2$, $B_1$, $B_2$. Start on the right with $B_2$.

Put $B_2$ under $B_1$ and under $A_2$, then bring back over $A_2$. Leave $B_2$ between $A_2$ and $B_1$.

Now take A$_1$ on the left.
Put A$_1$ under A$_2$ and under
B$_2$, then back over B$_2$.
Leave A$_1$ between A$_2$ and B$_2$.

A I →

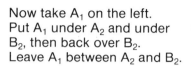

A2  AI  B2  BI

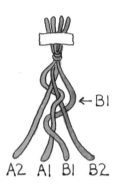

← BI

Now take B$_1$ and put it under
B$_2$ and under A$_1$, then back over
A$_1$. Leave B$_1$ between A$_1$ and B$_2$.

A2  AI  BI  B2

Pull the strings tightly after each
step. Keep braiding until the
bracelet is long enough to
go around your wrist.

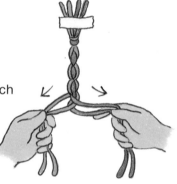

**5.** Tie the ends together with a knot.

**6.** Tie the two ends together to make the bracelet.